J Badger
Badger, H.
The alien brainwash /
$9.99

SCOUTING THE UNIVERSE FOR A NEW EARTH

WITHDRAWN

The Alien Brainwash
published in 2010 by
Hardie Grant Egmont
85 High Street
Prahran, Victoria 3181, Australia
www.hardiegrantegmont.com.au

*The pages of this book are printed on paper derived
from forests promoting sustainable management.*

All rights reserved. No part of this publication may be reproduced,
stored in a retrieval system or transmitted in any form by any means
without the prior permission of the publishers and copyright owner.

A CiP record for this title is available from the National Library of Australia.

Text copyright © 2010 H. Badger
Illustration and design copyright © 2010 Hardie Grant Egmont

Cover illustration by C. Stamation
Illustrated by C. Bennett
Series design by S. Swingler
Typeset by Ektavo
Printed in Australia by McPherson's Printing Group

1 3 5 7 9 10 8 6 4 2

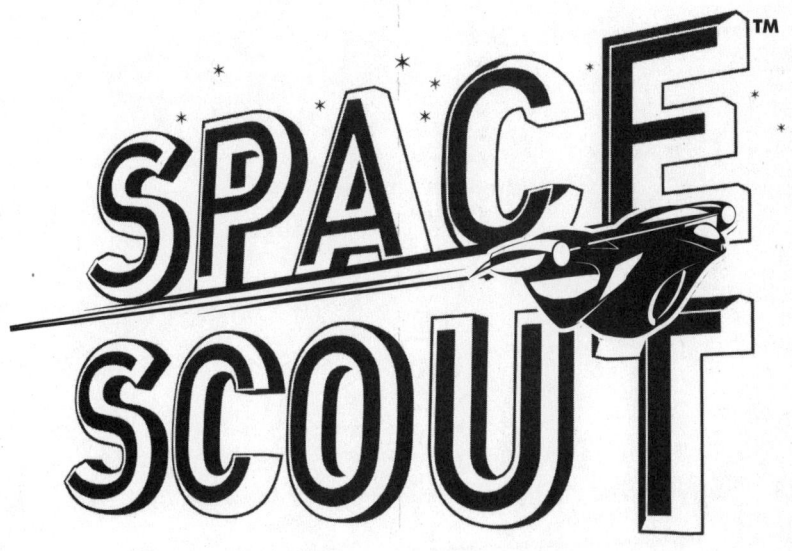

THE ALIEN BRAINWASH

BY **H. BADGER**
ILLUSTRATED BY **C. BENNETT**

hardie grant EGMONT

Kip Kirby couldn't believe it. His parents were *kissing*. In public! How embarrassing.

Gross! I wish I'd skipped this family outing, Kip thought to himself.

The Kirbys were visiting the Inner Eight Zoo. The zoo had native animals from all of the Milky Way's eight planets – Mercury, Venus, Earth, Mars, Jupiter, Saturn, Uranus and Neptune.

Except for when his parents were being disgusting, Kip loved the zoo. He was really into unusual animals. At home, Kip had a pet minisaur called Duke, a mini brontosaurus bred from fossil DNA. Dogs and cats hadn't been popular since 2200.

Kip didn't get much time to muck around with Duke. Firstly, he had school. Then there was Kip's job as a Space Scout.

Space Scouts explored deep space for another planet like Earth. The first Earth was running out of room, and so another one was needed quickly. The Milky Way's other planets were too hot, too cold or too gassy for humans.

Inner Eight Zoo

Kip followed his parents through the Inner Eight Zoo. The zoo was massive — it took up 400 floors of a building called the Titanium Tower. Instead of cages, the animals were inside huge, climate-controlled bubbles. Each had an atmosphere exactly like the animals' home planet.

'Oh, how gorgeous!' Kip's mum squealed. 'A little milk-weasel!'

Gorgeous? Try gross! Kip thought.

He wanted to go and check out the awesome fire panthers from Mercury. Six-legged fire panthers were hairless, with skin the colour of burnt sausages.

'The ring runners are on the 304th floor,' Kip's dad said, checking his holographic zoo guide. 'Let's have a look.'

Ring runners lived on Saturn's icy rings. They had tiny round bodies and long legs with four pairs of knees. Their top speed was over 250 kilometres per hour.

A ring runner's legs would be useful on Space Scout missions, Kip thought.

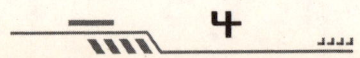

'How about we go and see the Insects On Uranus display first?' said Kip's mum.

'Sure,' Kip's dad replied cheerfully. 'There's a section about Killer Bug Flu, isn't there?'

Kip groaned silently. The insects from Uranus were great, but why did his parents have to make everything like school?

Kip's Teacherbot had been teaching his class about the Killer Bug Flu. Heaps of insect species in the outer galaxies had been wiped out, especially the bigger insects. Plants were at risk too. They needed insects to feed them and spread their seeds around.

Kip and his parents made their way through the crowded zoo. But just as they neared the insect display, Kip felt something on his wrist.

His SpaceCuff was buzzing!

The SpaceCuff was a thick silver band. It was an essential piece of scouting equipment. During missions, Kip used his SpaceCuff to communicate with his starship, MoNa 4000. When Kip got a message on Earth, it usually meant he had a new mission!

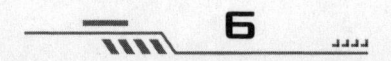

He grinned and checked his SpaceCuff.

SPACE SCOUT KIP KIRBY MISSION BRIEF

URGENT: RESCUE MISSION RECEIVED

Four days ago, Space Scout Zara Zadora went through a wormhole to a planet called Botanicus-1. All contact was suddenly lost when Zara entered Botanicus-1's orbit, and she hasn't been heard from since.

WorldCorp believes Zara's starship might have broken down. Even worse, foul play could be involved.

Your mission:

Go immediately to Botanicus-1 and find Zara.

A WorldCorp HandlerBot is waiting for you on the roof of the Zoo.

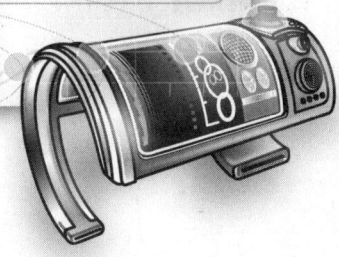

According to gossip, Zara was one of the top Space Scouts. It was an honour to be sent to rescue her. After all, Kip was only 12 years old – the youngest ever scout. He'd been chosen after scoring super high on tests of bravery, intelligence and physical strength.

Kip felt proud, but he was also a little disappointed. *This time my mission isn't exploring a planet*, he thought. *My ranking on the Planetary Points Leader Board will slip. And I could miss my shot at the Shield of Honour!*

Space Scouts earned one Planetary Point for exploring a planet. A promising discovery earned them two points. The scout who discovered the next Earth would win the ultimate prize – the Shield of Honour. The winner got the glory, plus a mansion on the new Earth with a rocket-skiing trip to Pluto thrown in.

Winning the shield would be awesome, Kip thought. *But rescuing Zara's a big deal, and it's a chance to prove myself to the other scouts.*

Kip looked around to say goodbye to his parents, but they had disappeared into the crowd. He messaged them instead.

They were used to Kip leaving suddenly on missions, so they wouldn't mind.

Kip wanted to get into space as soon as possible. No matter how many missions he went on, space travel was *always* exciting!

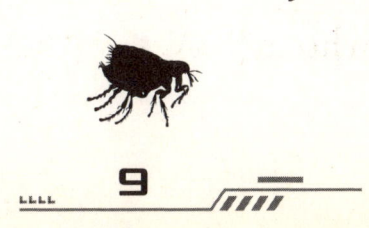

Just outside the insect display was a lift.

The ride to the roof took 0.1 seconds. Kip watched a MicroAd for his favourite snack on the lift's 3D TV.

Kip usually started missions by getting himself to the Intergalactic Hoverport. His starship MoNa was docked there. But this time, he had a ride.

When the lift doors opened, a squat, shiny green WorldCorp robot was waiting for Kip on the roof. It had red flashing eyes with buttons arranged in a smile. Beside the robot, Kip saw what looked like a giant two-metre-high spring.

'Greetings, Kip Kirby!' the robot chirped. It circled Kip's feet, herding him toward the spring. 'This will be FUN!'

Kip raised one eyebrow. The robot was obviously set to XTreme Positive mode. How annoying!

A section in the top of the robot's head flipped open. It took out a brand-new green spacesuit, helmet and spaceboots from inside, and then handed them to Kip.

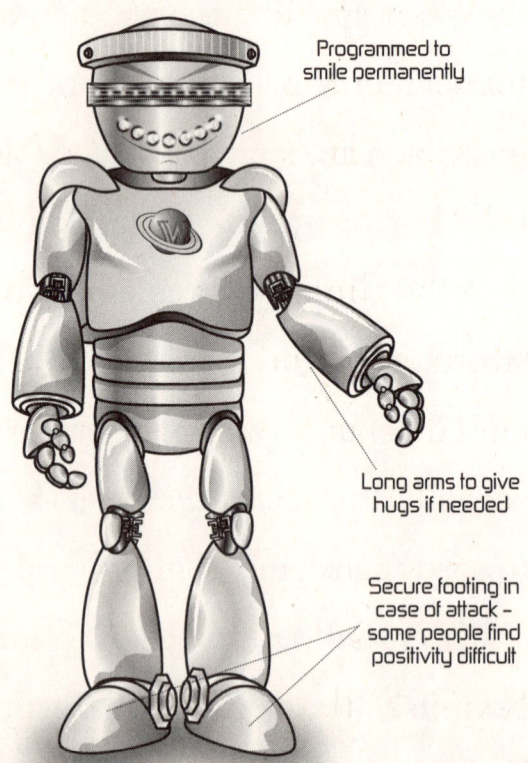

Programmed to smile permanently

Long arms to give hugs if needed

Secure footing in case of attack – some people find positivity difficult

WorldCorp Handlerbot: XTreme Positive mode

Kip didn't have his own space gear with him. He wasn't expecting to leave on a mission today!

As he suited up, Kip had a closer look at the giant spring. There were straps inside for each of Kip's wrists and ankles.

'Climb in and buckle up!' bleeped the robot.

Kip climbed into the spring and stretched out his arms and legs. The straps closed around his ankles and wrists. In a second, Kip was strapped inside the spring in a star-jump position.

'This is WorldCorp's all-new Space-Bounder,' the robot explained, its lights flashing excitedly. 'It's the latest innovation in environmentally friendly travel, and the fastest way to get to the Hoverport. Specially designed for urgent missions!'

Kip spotted a metal plaque screwed inside the spring.

WorldCorp SpaceBounder

1. SpaceBounder will be activated by your WorldCorp Handlerbot.
2. SpaceBounder will launch over the edge of the Inner Eight Zoo building.
3. SpaceBounder will hit Impact Zone on the ground below.
4. SpaceBounder will spring upwards into space.

Kip's eyes narrowed. His Space Scout training had taught him to question everything. Especially jumping off tall buildings!

The Impact Zone was a target painted on the ground. What if Kip missed and landed somewhere else? Someone could be seriously hurt. It sounded more dangerous than the mission itself!

It was a very long way down from the top of the building. Kip decided to ask the easiest question first. 'Er, how exactly will the SpaceBounder know when I've arrived at the Hoverport?'

'Relax!' chirped the robot. 'This Space-Bounder is designed so that someone your weight will spring up to the exact height of the Hoverport. The straps will automatically release when you arrive.'

The robot probably knows what it's doing, Kip told himself. *Doesn't it?*

'In testing, this prototype worked over 99 per cent of the time!' chirped the robot. 'Come on, hurry up!'

'Prototype?' Kip repeated. 'You mean, this thing isn't even –'

AAAHHHHH!

The SpaceBounder automatically launched Kip over the edge. Suddenly, he was plunging through mid-air!

The world rushed past Kip in a blur. His stomach flopped wildly and sweat poured down his forehead.

Kip caught a glimpse of people inside the zoo rushing to the windows. It wasn't every day that a Space Scout plummeted to the ground in a gigantic spring.

Kip had a highly trained eye for navigation. As he sped toward the ground, he saw at once that the SpaceBounder was off course.

I've gotta do something or else I'll miss the Impact Zone! he told himself.

There was no time for complicated calculations. Kip had to trust his gut. Heart hammering, he leant hard to the left. The SpaceBounder tipped sideways and rolled completely over eight times in a row.

Yes! It was just enough to line up perfectly with the Impact Zone.

SPROOOOINNGG!

The SpaceBounder hit the ground just inside the Impact Zone. *Lucky!*

Kip's bones rattled inside him as the SpaceBounder bounced upwards.

Next stop, the Hoverport, Kip thought, as the SpaceBounder hurtled past the Titanium Tower and into the sky.

Then on to Botanicus-1 to rescue Zara!

Kip whistled toward space inside the giant spring. The Hoverport loomed up above of him. It looked like a giant car park floating in the air. But instead of old-fashioned cars, starships of all shapes and sizes were docked there.

Kip's starship, MoNa, was docked in her usual spot. MoNa was a black multilevel starship with curved thrusters and a pointed nose cone.

The SpaceBounder is meant to automatically release me at the Hoverport, Kip remembered. But he still had to call MoNa and ask her to open her landing bay door to let him in.

My hands are strapped in, Kip thought. *So I can't reach my SpaceCuff to call!*

Kip hurtled closer and closer to MoNa. The harness began to release him. He was slipping out the bottom of the spring. At any moment, he could be free-falling through space – or worse, go **SPLAT** against the side of his starship!

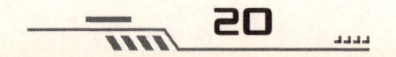

Just as he was about to slip out, Kip grabbed the bottom coil of the spring and clung on fiercely. 'MoNa!' he screamed, dangling in thin air.

As if MoNa had heard him, the landing bay door suddenly slid open. Kip felt the SpaceBounder being sucked toward his starship.

With MoNa's landing bay door just below him, Kip let go of the SpaceBounder and pin-dropped through it. He landed on the floor of the landing bay with a thud.

She must've used her MagnaSweep to pull in the spring! Kip thought, relieved.

The MagnaSweep was MoNa's high-powered magnet. It scanned the sky for dangerous metal debris. Or, in this case, for Space Scouts trapped inside giant springs!

MoNa 4000: MagnaSweep

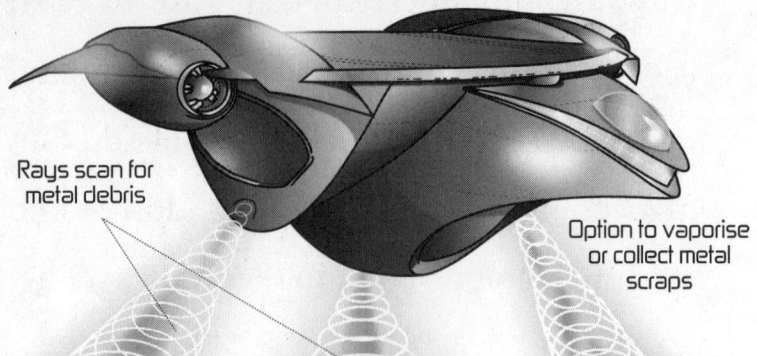

Rays scan for metal debris

Option to vaporise or collect metal scraps

'Thanks,' Kip said shakily.

'I really haven't got time for rescues,' came MoNa's cranky, computerised voice. 'I'm preparing to fly into deep space.'

Kip decided to change the subject. Sometimes MoNa got carried away thinking she was more important than him.

'Where's Finbar?' he asked.

Part-human and part-arctic wolf, Finbar

was an Animaul, created in case of alien invasion. But Finbar had failed Animaul training for being too gentle. He'd been made Kip's second-in-command instead.

'Try his sleep chamber,' MoNa said.

Puzzled, Kip left the landing bay.

I know Finbar likes daytime naps, Kip thought, barely noticing the dull rumble as MoNa left the Hoverport. *He IS part-wolf, and they're a kind of dog. But we're about to leave on a rescue mission!*

The door to Finbar's sleep chamber slid open and Kip poked his head inside.

Finbar was strapped into his wall-mounted vertical space bed. A dial on the pillow adjusted height and softness.

WorldCorp Vertical Space Bed

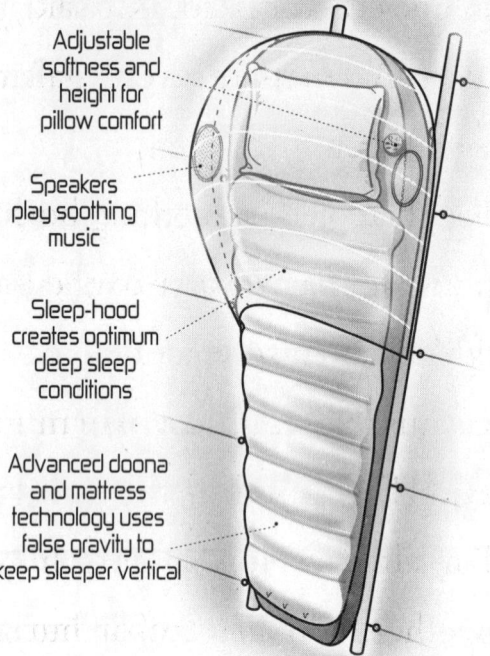

Adjustable softness and height for pillow comfort

Speakers play soothing music

Sleep-hood creates optimum deep sleep conditions

Advanced doona and mattress technology uses false gravity to keep sleeper vertical

Speakers on the sides played a selection of soothing music. Still, Finbar wasn't asleep. He looked miserable.

'Finbar, what's wrong?' Kip asked.

'I've got stinging space fleas,' Finbar groaned, itching his red tummy.

'Don't be embarrassed,' Kip said, giving him a pat. 'Animals in every galaxy get them sometimes.'

Finbar shrugged, scratching both ears.

'Kip and Finbar, report to the bridge,' chimed MoNa's crisp voice.

'She must've found a wormhole to Botanicus-1!' Kip said.

Finbar climbed down from his space bed. Together, Kip and Finbar hurried to the bridge, MoNa's command centre.

The bridge was in MoNa's nose cone. It had two giant windows looking out to space. A swirling mass of coloured clouds took up one whole window. The wormhole!

In the exact centre of the bridge were

two padded captains' chairs.

Sitting down, Kip swiped the air above his head. At once a cylinder of blue light shot down from above. MoNa's dials and controls were projected onto it.

Kip expertly touched a few keys on the holographic console. Immediately, MoNa shot forward into the wormhole.

Kip's skin prickled as though it was crawling with bugs, and his eyes bulged. Travelling light-years in a few seconds was convenient, but not very comfy.

Luckily, Finbar was too busy scratching a flea under his spacesuit to notice the wormhole. Normally, high-speed space travel made Finbar horribly space-sick.

MoNa popped out the other end of the wormhole. Directly ahead was a shimmering green planet. Excitement fizzed through Kip's veins. It always did when he saw a new planet for the first time.

Grabbing their helmets, Kip and Finbar raced to the landing bay. There, MoNa's Scrambler Beams would scramble their particles, beam them through space and rearrange them on Botanicus-1.

Kip jammed on his helmet. After one final nose scratch, Finbar did the same.

A pair of Scramblers shot down from the ceiling. Soon, Kip and Finbar's particles were shooting toward Botanicus-1.

It was finally time to find Zara!

CHAPTER 4

Kip and Finbar's particles reassembled themselves on Botanicus-1. Kip's first move was to check the Air Analyser on his SpaceCuff.

Air-Analyser mode

Pollen count: HIGH
Flying insects: NONE

The air was safe to breathe, so Kip took off his helmet. Flowery perfume filled the air, and he saw straight away why Botanicus-1 looked so green from space.

The entire planet was covered with rippling fields of flowers. Under Kip's feet, the soil was wet and silvery-green. A bright blue sun shone down from above.

'Smells like my granny's house,' said Kip, wrinkling his nose. He really wasn't into flowers.

Still, these flowers were cooler than most. They were taller than Kip, with identical tulip-shaped heads and thick, sticky stems dotted with claw-like retractable spikes.

They each had two leaves on their stems that moved like arms.

'Any sign of Zara?' Finbar asked, still scratching his fleas.

Kip shrugged.

The flowers were so tall that anything could be hidden in the field. Zara's wrecked starship, for example, or Zara herself. Kip could even see what looked like a shimmering, silver building in the distance. Was that a sign of alien life forms?

Suddenly, Kip felt a tap on the shoulder. He spun around, his heart thumping, and came face-to-face with a giant flower!

The flower's petals snapped open. Inside, a single black eye stared at Kip.

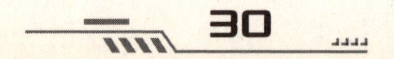

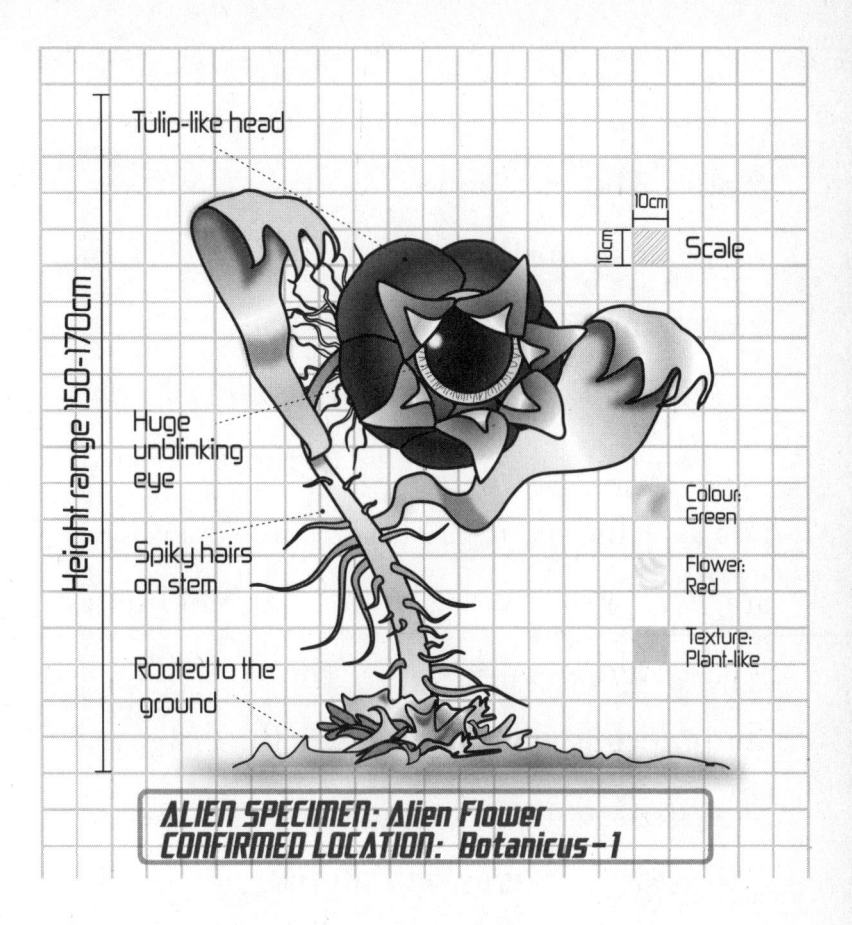

ALIEN SPECIMEN: Alien Flower
CONFIRMED LOCATION: Botanicus-1

- Tulip-like head
- Huge unblinking eye
- Spiky hairs on stem
- Rooted to the ground

Height range 150-170cm

Scale: 10cm × 10cm

Colour: Green
Flower: Red
Texture: Plant-like

A strange, soft sound drifted from the flower. It sounded like a cross between harp music and ghostly moaning.

'Is that flower…*talking*?' said Finbar.

Kip flicked his SpaceCuff to Translate mode. The translator used well-known alien languages to guess what new ones meant. It wasn't always reliable, but it could normally pick up a couple of words.

Translate mode:

**ERROR
UNABLE TO TRANSLATE**
No similar language in the universe.

TRANSLATOR

The flower was definitely talking. But just like Kip and Finbar, the Translate mode had never heard a language like *this* before.

Of course, the SpaceCuff had artificial

intelligence. Eventually it would learn to translate the flowers' language. But Kip didn't know how long that would take.

'The other flowers are talking to us too,' Finbar whispered. 'They're saying exactly the same thing at exactly the same time.'

They look like plants, Kip thought. *But if they're trying to talk to us, they must have brains.*

These aliens were very different to any Kip had seen before. They didn't seem to have houses or vehicles. They couldn't move around easily. And they all looked and spoke exactly the same way.

What does a flower being even eat? Kip thought. He had so many questions!

The nearby flowers leant in toward Kip and Finbar. They came closer and closer, making a circle. Kip felt their sticky leaves brushing his spacesuit.

'This doesn't feel friendly to me,' Kip muttered to Finbar.

The flowers began to sway. Their eerie, moaning voices filled the air.

Finbar yawned and stretched.

'You can't nap now!' Kip exclaimed.

CRASH!

Finbar had fallen face-first onto the ground! He was fast asleep.

Suddenly, Kip felt incredibly tired too. The field swam before his eyes. *I'll just lie down…for a minute…*he thought.

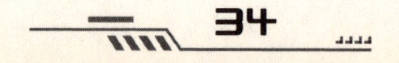

'Kip! *Kip!* Wake up!' whispered a voice in his ear.

Slowly, Kip opened one eye. Finbar's furry face was an inch away from Kip's.

'We fell asleep!' Finbar said. He scratched a flea bite behind his ear with his foot. 'Luckily, this itching woke me up.'

Kip snapped awake. The field was in darkness. The giant flowers had their petals closed, and their heads drooped like they were asleep. Soft rain was pattering down all around.

'How long were we asleep?' Kip whispered.

It had been day when they arrived, and now it was night. But every planet's day was a different length. A day on Botanicus-1 might last an Earth hour, or a whole Earth week!

Finbar shrugged.

'And why did we suddenly fall asleep in the middle of the day?' Kip added, feeling suspicious.

'I do that sometimes,' Finbar admitted.

'But *I* haven't had daytime naps since kindergarten!' Kip replied.

He remembered the circle of identical flowers. Their strange, musical language. Their single, unblinking eyes.

They're almost…hypnotic, Kip thought.

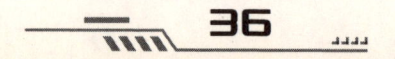

A chill of fear shot through him.

Kip suddenly had a very bad feeling about this mission.

There was a Space Scout missing on Bontanicus-1. Talking, thinking aliens that looked like flowers were all around them. And these flowers were anything but pretty.

CHAPTER 5

Kip thought for a moment, planning his next move. The flowers' hypnotic song had confused him. It looked like these flower-like aliens could be dangerous. But it also looked like they slept at night.

'I think night-time's our best chance to search Botanicus-1 for Zara,' he whispered to Finbar.

They'd have to search at top speed, since they didn't know how long the night would last. And they'd have to do it without waking the flowers.

The night was so dark and rainy that Kip couldn't see a thing. As quietly as possible, he rummaged in his backpack. He pulled a gadget from the very bottom.

A brand new UV-Trak!

The UV-Trak was a short, stubby wand with a UV light on the tip. The UV light picked up traces of a chemical called phosphorus. Every human had it in their body, and left traces of it behind.

Kip flicked the UV-Trak on. Immediately, a purple light trail blazed in the air behind him. It started near the ground, where Kip had woken up, and led to the spot where he was standing now.

'We can see where you've been,' said Finbar softly.

Waving the UV-Trak in front of them, Kip and Finbar tiptoed quickly through the field of sleeping flowers. Their spaceboots made no sound in the wet, silver soil.

They crept deeper into the field. Kip's eyes began to puff up and feel itchy.

'Pollen in the air,' Finbar whispered, scratching a flea bite. 'In fact, it's kind of odd – so much pollen, but no insects…'

But Kip was concentrating hard on finding Zara. He ran on ahead, waving the

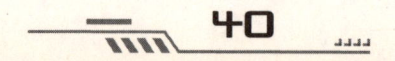

UV-Trak back and forth.

A faint purple trail appeared in the night air. Kip and Finbar rushed toward it. The trail blazed even brighter.

Zara's been here, Kip thought. *And by the look of that trail, she's close by!*

There was a large patch of bare, silvery sand just up ahead. Something about it looked wrong to Kip, and he stopped short. But before he could say anything, Finbar stepped right into the middle of it.

SQUELCH!

In the gloom, Kip could just make out Finbar's furry white shape disappearing into the silver soil.

Oh, no, Kip thought, trying not to panic.

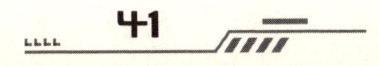

Quicksand!

He grabbed Finbar's paw and pulled as hard as he could. But Finbar was too heavy.

'I – can't – hold – you!' Kip's voice was strained with effort.

Finbar's shoulders sank beneath the soil. Then his neck disappeared to! And even though Kip was pulling as hard as he could, Finbar's paw was slipping away.

Kip clutched desperately at Finbar's paw. Then he remembered something.

'Your Hummingbird Pros!' Kip said. 'They're your only hope.'

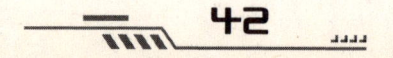

Kip and Finbar wore Hummingbird Pro spaceboots, which had carbon-fibre, water-repellent mini-turbo jets fitted to the sides of the heels.

Normally, they were used for flying in humid, zero-gravity conditions. But they might also be able to lift Finbar out of the quicksand.

Finbar kicked his legs to activate the jets. He gasped and spat out a mouthful of silver sand.

Kip pulled Finbar's wrists as hard as he could. The jets were just powerful enough to help drag Finbar upwards.

'Almost there!' Kip panted.

With one final, massive effort, Kip hauled Finbar out of the quicksand. The force sent Kip stumbling backwards.

KER-RUNCH!

Kip's foot landed with a sickening crunch on something. He glanced around, worried that he might have woken the flowers. But it looked like they were still asleep.

With a deep breath, Kip glanced down.

If he didn't have heaps of experience staying cool in creepy situations, he would have screamed.

Kip had stepped on a gigantic bug!

It had six bulging eyes, eight black furry legs, razor-sharp fangs and a metre-long sting.

Kip tore his foot off the massive bug

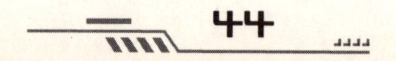

like it was burning hot. He didn't know if it was still alive, but he wasn't waiting to find out!

'The spiderbee can't harm you now,' said a smooth, calm voice. 'It's dead – just like all the others.'

Kip whipped around. In front of him stood a woman dressed in a green spacesuit just like Kip and Finbar's. She had blonde hair and violet eyes with a blank, faraway look in them.

Kip recognised her from her Planetary Points Leader Board photo.

It was Zara Zadora!

CHAPTER 6

'Kip Kirby, Space Scout,' Kip said, sticking out his hand.

Kip knew all about Zara from Space Scout gossip. This was the first time they'd actually met.

'We're here to rescue you,' Finbar said.

Zara blinked slowly, but she didn't take Kip's hand. 'You want to rescue me?'

Her eyes had a glazed look, as though she didn't understand.

'Yes!' said Kip, raising an eyebrow. 'You're a Space Scout, like me. You work for WorldCorp. You're supposed to be finding the next Earth, remember?'

Zara's expression was still blank. 'I only serve the Beautiful Ones,' she said softly. 'They're the wondrous beings of Botanicus-1.'

'I suppose she means the flowers,' Finbar whispered to Kip. 'You wouldn't call those dead bugs *beautiful*.'

Kip stared at Zara, his mind racing. How could Zara break the first rule of Space Scouting so carelessly?

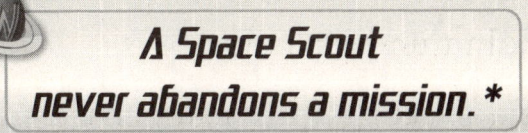

> **A Space Scout never abandons a mission.***
>
> *Even when being slimed by an angry alien.

No Space Scout in her right mind would do that! he thought.

But then again, maybe Zara *wasn't* in her right mind.

Kip reached into his backpack. He had a theory. And he knew just the gadget to test it out. WorldCorp's Disco Disc!

The Disco Disc was the size of an old-fashioned 20-cent piece, money that people had used centuries ago. When snapped in half, it released powerful flashing lights.

It also sprayed white smoke and pumped old-fashioned disco music.

The Disco Disc was supposed to help Space Scouts break the ice with stand-offish aliens on new planets. When WorldCorp had tested it on humans, they found that it was impossible to resist the urge to dance to the Disco Disc. If Zara was completely with it, she'd *have* to dance.

The only problem with the plan was that it might wake up the flowers. But Kip was running out of options. Hopefully the flowers were heavy sleepers. The sun was almost up and they would wake up soon anyway.

Kip snapped the disc in half. At once,

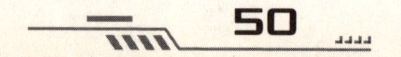

flashing lights and music pumped into the night air. Kip's feet started tapping and he spun around to the catchy beat. He looked over at Finbar, whose human side couldn't resist bobbing along too. But when Kip looked at Zara, she was still staring blankly into space without moving.

Kip shook his head grimly. He turned off the Disco Disc quickly, glancing around at the still-sleeping flowers.

'Just as I thought!' he whispered to Finbar. 'She's been hypnotised, or brain-washed or something.'

'Well, she should be very open to suggestions,' said Finbar. 'We could command her to come home with us!'

'Good idea,' Kip said. 'As long as we can figure out how to break the hypnosis back on Earth. I'll dial MoNa and get her to send down three Scrambler Beams.'

DIALLING .... MoNa 4000

ERROR – No response

Why isn't she answering? Kip thought, his forehead wrinkling with worry.

'The Beautiful Ones ordered your starship out of the sky,' murmured Zara.

'*What?*' Kip said.

'That's what happened to my starship,' smiled Zara. 'There she is, over there.'

Kip could just see a starship's nose

cone sticking out of the silver soil. One side was almost buried under a mound of dead spiderbees. The gross bugs were everywhere.

Kip shivered. If MoNa was wrecked and they couldn't contact her, it meant they were stranded!

Sooner or later, he'd have to solve that problem. But at that moment, he had something even *worse* to deal with.

Dawn was breaking, and the flowers were waking up!

Kip wasn't giving them the chance to hypnotise him and Finbar all over again.

Kip's brain churned. He hadn't been able to talk to the flowers and explain his situation. They were living, thinking creatures just like he was. Maybe if they understood why Kip needed Zara back, they'd let her go.

It didn't seem likely. The flowers had been nothing but creepy so far. But it was worth a shot!

Kip flicked his SpaceCuff to Translate mode. The chip inside was very powerful. By now, it should have worked out some of the flowers' strange language.

The flowers began talking in their musical voices, perfectly in time with each other.

Kip checked the translation on his SpaceCuff screen.

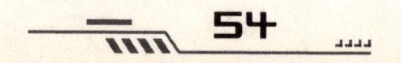

Translate mode:
Flowerspeak to English

One worker good. Three even better.

The flowers hypnotised Zara so she'd work for them! Kip guessed. *Now they want us to do the same. But what job are we supposed to do?*

Kip felt a sticky stem winding around his legs. Leaves rustled against his spacesuit. The flowers were closing in again. Kip tried to find a gap in the circle of flowers around them, but there was no way through.

The flowers' musical language filled the air. Finbar yawned, and Kip fought to keep focused. The hypnosis was starting again!

Desperately, Kip punched his question

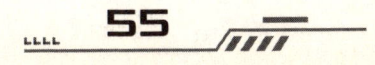

into his SpaceCuff. He hoped it could translate from English to Flowerspeak.

Translate mode:
English to Flowerspeak

What job do you want us to do? Is there another solution? Zara is needed on Earth.

ERROR: Translation failed

The SpaceCuff hadn't totally finished learning Flowerspeak. Kip couldn't make the flowers understand him!

The flowers continued their eerie song. Kip struggled as hard as he could, but his eyes were slowly closing. *I've…got…to…stay…awake!* he thought desperately. *But how?*

CHAPTER 7

'The Beautiful Ones are hypnotising you again,' Zara said dreamily. 'And if you're hypnotised long enough, you'll be brainwashed forever.'

At once, every cell in Kip's body snapped awake. 'Brainwashed forever?' he yelled. 'How long do we have to be hypnotised before that happens?'

'A while for highly trained people like Space Scouts,' Zara replied. 'With others, well... you just never know.'

She looked at Finbar. His eyelids were lowering.

Finbar's wolf hearing is extra-sensitive! Kip realised. *He fell asleep before me last time. And he hasn't had all the special Space Scout anti-hypnosis training I've had.*

Still, Kip knew even he couldn't resist the flowers forever. He had to stay awake – and make sure Finbar did too.

When did I last feel super-awake? he asked himself.

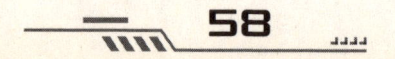

It was during Space Scout training. Those vertical wall sprints and rocketbootassisted high jumps had been tough.

I couldn't have done it without EarTunes!

EarTunes were songs played directly into the eardrum. All Space Scouts had EarTunes chips implanted in their earlobes on the first day of training.

Kip gave his earlobe three firm squeezes. At once, 'Space Rambler' by the Screeching UFOs flooded his brain. Since it was played inside Kip's head, only he could hear it.

Flying through the stars, shooting straight through space, I am a SPACE RAMBLER!

It totally blocked out the flowers' eerie song, waking him up faster than a cold slime shower.

Now the only problem was Finbar. He didn't have EarTunes because he was 2iC, not a Space Scout.

'Just...gonna...rest...for a...while...' Finbar muttered, sinking to the ground.

'No!' yelled Kip, shaking Finbar's arm to keep him awake.

But Finbar didn't answer.

Waving his arms, Kip rushed toward Finbar. The flowers shrank back in surprise.

'Wake up!' Kip yelled desperately.

There was a snuffling sound from Finbar's wet black nose. Then...

Finbar opened his eyes. They were normally a piercing pale blue. They looked different to Kip now. Softer somehow.

'I want to serve the Beautiful Ones,' Finbar said slowly. 'Where do I begin?'

Finbar had only been asleep for a second. Was he brainwashed already?

I've got to test him! Kip thought. *Finbar said earlier that brainwashed people are easy to order around.*

'Finbar, I want you to purr like a cat,' Kip said, trying to keep his voice steady. Finbar *really* hated cats.

But instantly, Finbar started purring loudly. He even rubbed his paws on his head, like a cat cleaning its ears!

He really is hypnotised, Kip thought miserably. *Although...*

For a second, Kip thought Finbar had winked at him. But when he looked closer, all he saw were Finbar's glazed eyes.

I guess I saw what I wanted to see, Kip thought.

He needed a plan. With his EarTunes playing, he was safe from the flowers' hypnotic powers. But he had to work out how to save Finbar and Zara!

Zara linked arms with Finbar. The

flowers swayed apart. Zara led Finbar away through the field.

Kip raced after them. He didn't want to lose Zara and Finbar in the huge field. With a brainwashed 2iC and no way to contact MoNa, Kip was on his own.

Maybe if the flowers think I'm already under their spell, he thought suddenly, *they'll stop trying to hypnotise me.*

'I want to serve the Beautiful Ones too!' Kip said slowly, trying to make his eyes glaze over like Finbar's.

Zara and Finbar turned slowly and waited for Kip to catch up, then the three of them continued across the field.

Kip hadn't noticed before, but the field

sloped downwards toward the middle.

Zara was definitely heading for something in particular. Something in the very centre of the field that was hidden behind the tall flowers in the field.

It looked like the shimmering silver structure Kip had glimpsed when they first landed on Botanicus-1.

He had no idea what the building was or what would be inside. But he desperately hoped it would help him unlock the flowers' secrets and figure out how to get Zara and Finbar home.

CHAPTER 8

Kip, Zara and Finbar were standing in a clearing in the middle of the field. There were only a few flowers nearby.

In the clearing stood the shimmering dome-shaped building. It was almost transparent, glittering in the blue sunlight. It was a bit taller than the flowers, and very long.

'First, we must harvest the golden grains,' Zara was explaining.

She tapped a nearby flower on the stem. The flower leant down. It shook its head into Zara's cupped hands. Tiny specks of yellow pollen tumbled from the centre of the flower. Zara caught every speck like it was gold dust.

With a frozen smile, Finbar tapped another flower. He collected the pollen grains in his white, furry paw. For a moment, Kip thought he saw Finbar give his leg a quick scratch with his foot.

But then Finbar smiled blankly and said, 'I love serving the Beautiful Ones.'

Kip gagged. He wanted the old Finbar back! Still, he tapped a flower and collected some pollen himself. He had to pretend he was brainwashed too – as well as use his Space Scout logic to figure out what was happening on Botanicus-1.

When all three had their hands full, Zara led them into the shimmering building.

Kip touched the side of the building.

Up close, he saw it was made of billions of criss-crossing threads. It felt sticky, like the silk that was spun by insects.

They stepped inside the building through an arched doorway. Inside, Kip saw an almost endless stretch of silvery green soil. Growing in perfect rows were more flowers the size of seedlings.

'This is the greenhouse,' Zara beamed.

She guided them toward the nearest flower. Carefully, she dropped a single speck of pollen into its petals.

Finbar followed. But his wolf paws were clumsy. A pollen speck tumbled from his grip.

Zara dived to catch it before it hit the

dirt. 'The golden grains are precious!' she squeaked. 'Without them, the Beautiful Ones cannot survive.'

Kip had a photographic memory for details, even nerdy ones. It was one reason why he was such a talented Space Scout. The golden specks reminded him of something his Teacherbot had told him.

Zara and Finbar are taking pollen from the outside flowers to the young flowers inside the greenhouse, he thought. Kip knew that insects normally did that job.

His mind was racing at warp speed. *I bet those weird giant spiderbees used to spread the pollen*, he thought. *They could have made this greenhouse too.*

Zara had said that the spiderbees were all dead now. But back when dawn was breaking, Kip had noticed that the bodies littered on the ground hadn't started decomposing yet. That could only mean that the spiderbees had died recently.

Then Kip had a brainwave. *Maybe the Intergalactic Killer Bug Flu wiped them out!*

It meant that the flowers needed someone else to do the spiderbees' job. Because the flowers couldn't really walk, they couldn't spread their pollen to the little flowers inside the greenhouse! And without the pollen, new flowers couldn't grow.

So the flowers hynotised Zara, and then Finbar, to spread the pollen for them!

Kip had to admit that it was pretty clever.

A loud rumble outside interrupted Kip's whirring brain. A fork of fizzing orange lightning lit up the sky. Rain started pouring down.

Finbar's doggy side hated thunderstorms! Kip was sure that if he wasn't brainwashed, he'd be terrified.

Kip watched Finbar closely. Zara kept on pollinating seedlings. But Finbar had stopped what he was doing. The fur on the back of his neck stood on end. His glazed smile drooped.

Outside, another lightning fork sizzled across the sky. Finbar's ears flattened again his head. He let out a low, mournful growl.

Kip's Space Scout training had taught him that things weren't always what they seem. When Zara was a safe distance away, he walked over to Finbar.

'You'll be fine,' Kip whispered. 'It's just a thunderstorm.'

Finbar looked Kip in the eye. 'Thanks,' he whispered back.

Finbar's voice sounded completely normal. He hadn't even mentioned serving the Beautiful Ones!

Relief flooded though Kip. *Finbar's only faking being hypnotised! We had the same idea.*

Kip had been right about the wink. But what about the cat-like purrs?

'For a giant walking cottonball, you're a pretty good actor,' Kip muttered.

Finbar grinned and scratched his leg.

At that moment, Zara wondered over.

'Let's gather more golden grains,' Finbar told her, acting brainwashed again.

Zara reached out to take Finbar's paw. Just at that moment, a stinging space flea flew out from Finbar's spacesuit and landed on Zara.

Zara didn't seem to notice, but suddenly Kip had an idea.

It was pretty out-there. But then again, so was this entire mission.

CHAPTER 9

Kip's plan was weird, but simple.

Botanicus-1 needs insects. Finbar's got too many. Finbar's stinging space fleas could be trained to pollinate the flowers!

'The Botanicus-1 flowers need us, so let's go,' Kip commanded.

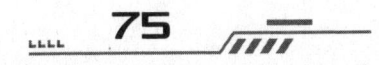

The brainwashed Zara followed obediently as Kip and Finbar raced out of the greenhouse, through the clearing and back into the flower field. As he ran, Kip flicked on his SpaceCuff and typed.

Translate mode:
English to Flowerspeak

Attention flowers

He hoped the SpaceCuff had finished learning to translate by now. Kip watched the screen nervously. Then…

A translation popped up! But instead of words, Kip had to sing a series of musical notes so that the flowers could understand him.

A Space Scout's got to be ready for anything,

Kip thought, clearing his throat. *Even a spot of opera!*

'My 2iC is infested with fleas,' Kip warbled at the flowers in his best high-pitched moan. 'Hypnotise them instead of us. They'll do the spiderbees' job!'

The flowers rustled. They understood!

Kip held his breath as the field was silent. They seemed to be deciding whether Kip's plan could work.

At last, the nearest flowers bent down and sang their reply. 'The flowers love the idea!' Kip said, reading the translation from his Space-Cuff. 'They never wanted to keep anyone prisoner. They just needed a way to pollinate their seedlings.'

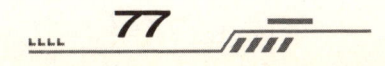

The flowers looked a bit like the ones on Earth. But Kip knew they were more complex than any flower back home. The flowers had a language, for a start, and they seemed to have emotions like humans and aliens, too.

The flowers near Finbar set to work on the fleas at once. They swayed left to right in perfect time with each other.

The flowers rubbed their leaf arms together above their heads as they swayed. Their voices joined together in song, so high-pitched that only the fleas could hear it properly.

Fleas streamed out the neck of Finbar's spacesuit. The faster the flowers sang and swayed, the more excited the fleas got. Soon the air was thick with space fleas, flying in formation.

'It's working!' Kip yelled. 'The fleas are brainwashed.'

'Hang on,' said Finbar suddenly. 'My fleas are tiny and the spiderbees were massive. It'll take the fleas ages to do the spiderbees' job.'

Kip grinned. 'I thought of that,' he said, reaching for the Yum X-Pander gadget tucked into the pocket of his spacesuit.

Space Scouts used Yum X-Panders when food supplies were short on missions. X-Panders shot a ray that took tasty food particles and multiplied them thousands of times. A normal donut could grow as big as a tyre in half a second.

Kip aimed the Yum X-Pander at the cloud of fleas. He squeezed the trigger. A bright yellow ray shot out. There was a flash and then the faint smell of singed fleas.

Instantly, the fleas grew to the size of Kip's head. He fired the Yum X-Pander again until the fleas were as big as the

Original donut is normal size

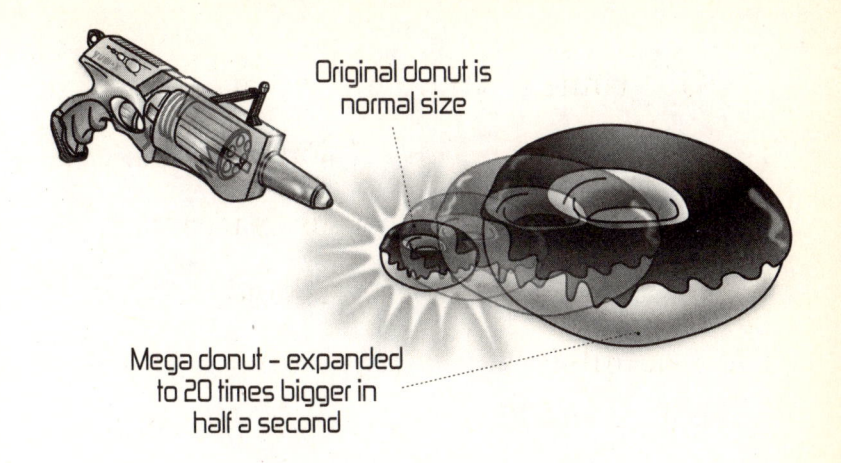

Mega donut - expanded to 20 times bigger in half a second

WorldCorp Yum X-Pander

spiderbees had been.

At that size, the fleas' creepy pincers, giant bulging eyes and fuzzy wings were very easy to see.

Finbar shuddered. '*That's* what was crawling all over me?'

But the flowers were thrilled. They started singing again to Kip and Finbar.

'To thank us, they're going to reverse

Giant Stinging Space Flea

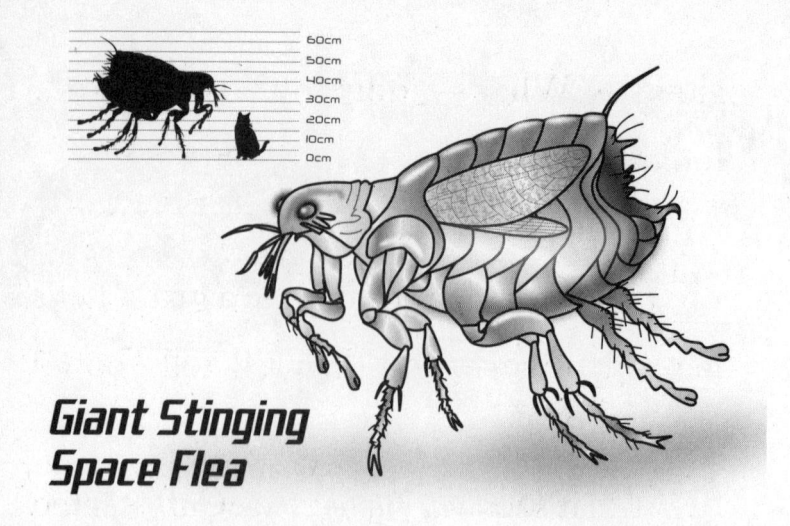

our brainwashing,' Kip translated, looking down at his SpaceCuff. Then he winked at Finbar. No point in telling the flowers that they'd only been pretending!

The flowers began swaying in the opposite direction. They struck up their song again, lower-pitched and with the strange tune reversed.

A moment later, Zara shook her head

slowly. 'What's going on?' she asked, looking confused.

Her hypnosis was broken!

'Long story,' said Kip with a grin. 'Let's get out of here, and then I'll tell you all about it.'

At that second, Kip's SpaceCuff started buzzing impatiently.

Incoming call... MoNa

Kip punched the Call Answer button.

'At last,' MoNa said grumpily. 'I've tried to call you three times.'

'What?' Kip said. 'I've been trying to call *you*. I thought you were wrecked!'

'Hmmph,' MoNa sniffed. 'Well, there

has been a lot of strange musical interference in the atmosphere.'

Kip sighed with relief. 'I think we've sorted that out,' he said. 'Can you send us three Scramblers? And you'll need to use your MagnaSweep to take Zara's wrecked starship back home for repairs.'

The second the Scrambler Beams appeared, Kip, Finbar and Zara stepped into them. Kip felt the familiar sensation of his body parts being shuffled by a giant pair of invisible hands.

Moments later, Kip, Finbar and Zara were safely back in MoNa's landing bay.

Kip's mission was complete…almost.

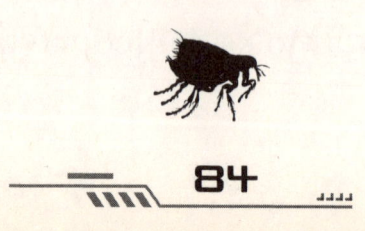

CHAPTER 10

'Time to file your mission report,' said MoNa bossily.

Kip glanced at Zara. It was strange having another Space Scout on board, especially a more experienced one. Would Zara think MoNa ordered Kip around just because he was young?

'Don't worry,' Zara whispered to Kip.

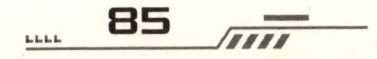

'Starships think they know everything, but they'd be nothing without us.'

Kip grinned. Zara seemed to think he was a top Space Scout, even if he was the youngest.

Together, they all made their way to the bridge. Kip sat down in his captain's chair. Immediately, his holographic console appeared around him.

Exploring Botanicus-1 had been Zara's mission. But during her rescue, Kip had seen a lot of the planet. So he could tell WorldCorp whether Botanicus-1 could be the next Earth.

He went straight to the File Mission Report screen and began to type.

CAPTAIN'S LOG
Botanicus-1

Population: Giant flowers. They can communicate and seem to have thoughts and feelings.

Like: Singing in harmony. Their songs have the power to hypnotise and eventually brainwash listeners.

Environment: Both rainy and sunny. The environment was perfect for growing flowers...until the Killer Bug Flu struck, killed the spiderbees and threw everything off balance.

Animals: As of ten minutes ago, a population of giant stinging space fleas. Space fleas exist in all known galaxies so they're unlikely to harm the ecosystem of Botanticus-1.

> **Recommendation:** I can't recommend Bontanicus-1 as Earth 2. The planet needs time to adjust to its new giant flea population. Plus, kids would go crazy with nothing to do hang out with singing flowers all day.

KIP KIRBY, SPACE SCOUT #50

CLASSIFIED

Sighing, Kip sent off his report. He'd completed his mission, but he probably wouldn't get a Planetary Point this time. It had been a rescue mission, not a scouting one.

He clicked on the latest Space Scout leader board. *I'll be right down the bottom,* he thought glumly. But when the board finished down-loading, Kip gasped.

Space Scout Leader Board

#1 Blake Nagoda

#2 Danika Treasure

#3 Kip Kirby*

* For accepting and completing a rescue mission without complaint, 2 honorary Planetary Points awarded.

Kip flushed with pride. Getting on with the rescue mission without making a fuss was definitely the right decision.

'I'm scanning for wormholes to Earth,' announced MoNa. 'It might be a while before one opens up.'

Kip shrugged. He was in no hurry to get home. What if his parents had another family outing in mind?

'Let's show Zara the Hobbytron,' Kip suggested quickly.

MoNa might have been grumpy, but she made up for it with cool new features like the Hobbytron.

The Hobbytron was shaped like a huge upside-down bowl. A digital display seemed to float on its glossy black sides.

Kip, Finbar and Zara stepped inside. 'I'll set it to Random Hobby,' Kip said, adjusting the controls.

MoNa 4000: Hobbytron

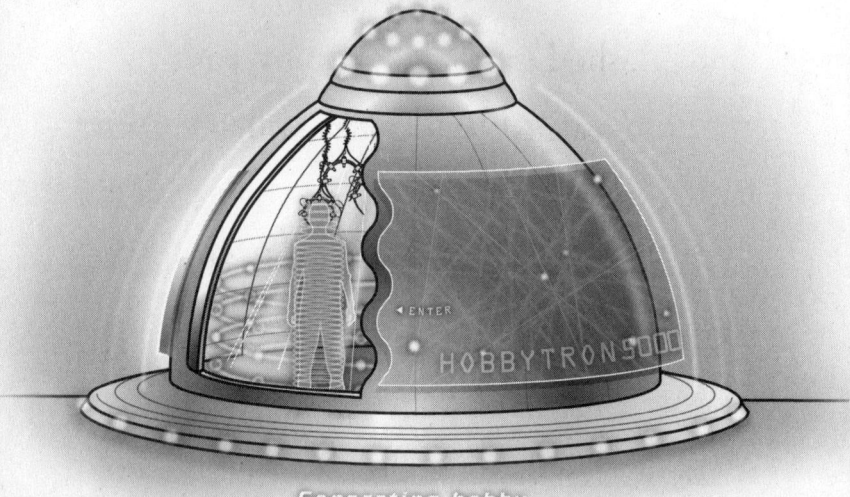

Generating hobby

Flower arranging   **Laser-sword duelling**   **Alien bug collecting**   **Trick hoverboarding**

'Cool,' said Zara. 'My starship doesn't have one of these! What do I do?'

'Stick these on your head,' Kip told Zara. He pointed to a bunch of electrodes dangling from the roof.

They stuck their electrodes on. At once, lights flashed inside the Hobbytron.

'Generating hobby…' said a smooth digital voice.

Suddenly, a powerful smell of flowers filled the Hobbytron. Virtual reality flowers sprang up all around.

Kip leant down and tried to pick one. Although it was digital, a thorn on the stem pricked him. Kip started bleeding! Virtual reality was getting more real every day.

'Today's random hobby is…flower arranging,' said the Hobbytron voice.

Kip and Zara rolled their eyes at each other. As if two top Space Scouts would spend their time off practising flower arranging! Anyway, they'd had more than enough flowers for one mission.

'What about extreme trick hoverboarding instead?' Zara said.

'As long as we set the skill level to "death defying",' Kip agreed.

Finbar's ears went flat. 'I might sit this one out,' he said, shaking his head.

Kip grinned at him. Some things were best enjoyed by Space Scouts only!

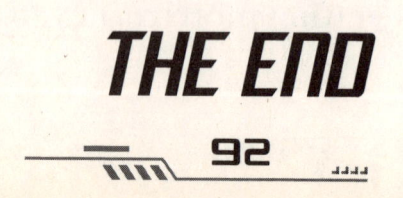

THE END